MAGE, MAZE, DEMON

CHARLES ALLEN GRAMLICH

Based
on the
dream
journals of
KYLE J. KNAPP

Praise for Charles Allen Gramlich's
MAGE, MAZE, DEMON ...

Mage Maze Demon ... is a short story that delivers the uber-fast adventure pulp fiction readers expect.

—S.E. Lindberg
Author and reviewer of Sword and Sorcery fiction

* * *

[Gramlich] spins a heck of a yarn, and I feel he's at his best when his main character has a sword in his fist. This was fun.

—Chris La Tray
Writer and photographer at chrislatray.com

* * *

Gramlich's prose goes down very smooth, with some nice imagery and new takes on the tropes of barbarian, sorcerer, and demon. Bryle, the protagonist, is more thoughtful than most characters of his type.

—Garnett Elliott
Author of *Red Venus* and *Dragon by the Bay*

CONTENTS

BONUS STORIES:

In another world ...

MAGE, MAZE, DEMON

1

The most vicious of all predators hunts in the forest. The barbarian flees. His name is Bryle. He dodges standing trees, leaps fallen logs, bulls past thorns and briars. A trio of gray wolves runs as well. They swiftly pull ahead. Bryle picks up the pace, though dares not run himself to exhaustion—as the wolves are doing. The wolves will tire; the thing that hunts them all will not.

Birds startle away through the trees. Deer race past. Bryle spots something on the ground ahead. He plucks it up. It's a tortoise. Its black eyes goggle; its legs still move though its feet don't touch the earth. He tucks it inside his rawhide vest where its claws scratch harmlessly. Finally, he glances over one shoulder.

It is fire that hunts. The forest roils with flames. Tendrils of crimson and orange whirl between the trees like the churning legs of a giant. Sap explodes into a shrapnel of embers, lashing Bryle now to the greatest effort he can muster. Sweat slimes him. His chest heaves. He passes a wolf from earlier. It staggers, bloody froth at its muzzle. Its heart must be near rupturing. Nothing can be done.

Bryle bursts into a meadow. The dry grass is taller than his head. No god of fire could wish for better tinder. Seed husks and pollen shower him as he runs, clinging to sweat-wet skin. A cliff rises ahead and he angles along it. Another rock face appears but there is a gap between the two and he takes it.

The open lane narrows and the constricting wind drives the flames into a frenzy. They eat the grass and brush with relentless speed. Smoke overtakes him and he coughs and chokes. Human muscles begin to falter, human sinews to scream. Out of the pall looms canyon's end. Sheer rock lifts over dead cedars that will make perfect fodder for fire. No exit! The flames shriek with joy like a fiend.

2

Then Bryle glimpses a crack in the cliff that gives him hope. It starts just above his head, zigzags up to a ledge that might hold him. Bryle draws his knives, the only weapons he hasn't discarded. He leaps and buries one knife blade into the crack. Smoke gags him. His boots scrabble at the cliff, find some purchase. He slams the second knife into the crack higher up.

Flames caress him, filling him with maniacal strength. He gets his right foot onto the hilt of the bottom knife. His left foot finds the second hilt. It slips and he hurls himself upward. Desperate fingers clutch the promising ledge.

The fire roars like a coliseum crowd. The heat is intense. Bryle's fingers dig at stone. He powers upward, rolls onto the ledge and away from the burning air. A cave looms dark and cool. He looks back at the hungry flames, sees a devil's face with a snarling mouth and a hundred flickering tongues that lick out to take his life. He scrambles into the cave; fire follows on the wind.

The flames grab for him but find nothing to feed on and ebb away. Bryle collapses, wracked with coughing. The fire leaves a vestige behind. On the cave walls are cressets holding torches. Now some of those torches are lit.

A rumbling assaults Bryle's ears. Dust puffs down around him. The sound stops; dust settles. Where the exit had been, now stands a smooth wall of stone. For a moment, all Bryle feels is relief at being shut away from the fire. Then something claws his chest and he cries out. His hand finds the tortoise and fresh relief fills him. He laughs uproariously. He is safe.

So he thinks.

3

In the moment after blessed relief sweeps through Bryle, questions boil up. Who sealed the door to this cave? Why? Was it to keep out the fire? Or to keep him in?

Plucking one lit torch from its cresset, Bryle inspects the sealed doorway. He sees no latch or anything else that might open it. He'll have to find another way. The cave extends deeper into the mountain and he turns to explore it. Only occasionally must he duck. The way is downward and he does not like that. Most of his life has been lived under open sky.

A glow blooms ahead and he soon comes out in a much larger cavern where late morning sunbeams fall through a broad hole high in the ceiling. A stream runs through the cavern and the scent of living things fills his nostrils. Beneath the sunlight grow moss and bushes and a tough, wiry grass. Bryle kneels to drink and the water is sweet. He fills the water skin at his belt and stoppers it. Upon rising again, he realizes he's not alone.

In the shadows to one side of the cavern, a figure sits on a broken throne. Bryle hoists his torch and the light reveals an eyeless man dressed in glass armor. The man's face is turned toward Bryle, though his eyes are no more than black holes. He smiles when the torch reveals him, and for an instant flames burn deep within his sockets.

"It is fortunate that you proved worthy of survival," the man says.

"Fortunate for who?" Bryle asks.

"For us both."

Bryle studies the man a bit, then guesses: "*You* closed the cavern door."

A small nod signifies the man's agreement.

"Did you also start the fire?"

Another nod.

"So you tried to kill me. Then saved me?"

"I tested you. And found you acceptable."

Bryle bristles. "Perhaps I should test you in turn."

The man chuckles loudly. "Barbarians and their pride."

Bryle lets a faint smile curve his lips. "Sorcerers and their theatrics."

The sorcerer stops laughing.

"So what is it you want from me?" Bryle asks.

The sorcerer brings his palms together in front of his face. "We in the brotherhood have a rule," he says. "Never call up that which you cannot put down."

"And you failed to follow that nugget of wisdom?"

"Not completely at least."

"You want me to put it down for you."

"If I cannot, you cannot. But still you can help me."

"How?"

The sorcerer waves a hand toward a doorway in the far wall of the cavern.

"Beyond that door waits a maze I constructed ages ago for protection," the sorcerer explains. "At its center is a white room. Within it—a talisman I can use against the demon I conjured. Most defenses for the maze ward against sorcery, and now the demon is in position to use them. It cannot escape; I cannot enter without being discovered. *You*, however. The evil one will not be expecting you."

"So, I retrieve the talisman. Bring it back. What then?"

"I open the way for you to leave this place. I use the talisman to put down the demon. My life, and yours, go on as before."

"You said 'most' of the defenses were set to balk sorcery. Not all?"

"Three lines of protection are physical. First, just beyond this cavern lies a flooded tunnel. Beneath the surface are three openings. Two are blind corridors leading to death; one takes you farther into the maze. That one is not always in the same position but its water is always hot.

"Second, there are many physical traps within the maze. Poisoned darts. Falling spears. Other things. But in the first chamber you come to after the water there is a secret to disarm them all."

"And what is that secret?"

The sorcerer shrugs. "That depends on whether the demon has changed it or not. It won't be expecting a physical attack so perhaps it has not."

"Comforting," Bryle says. "What *was* the secret?"

"Three statues. On bases that rotate. The first one in the chamber should face directly away from the other two, which should face each other."

"How will I know if that pattern still works?"

"If the first trap doesn't kill you."

Bryle arches an eyebrow. "And the third physical defense?"

"A beast. Black furred. Black clawed. It roams at will in the maze. There are sorcerous elements about it. It heals quickly. It's always hungry but does not need food to live. But it can be killed with non-sorcerous weapons."

"I lost my weapons in the fire."

"There are plenty of others free for taking in the maze. You will not be the first human to venture within." The sorcerer smiles. "The others did not have my guidance."

"The maze itself. Have you a map?"

"A map would do no good. The maze ... shifts. You will have to find your own way through."

"It appears your 'guidance' isn't worth as much as you think it is."

Again the sorcerer shrugs.

"And the talisman?" Bryle asks.

"An eye. In a vial protected by a spell the demon cannot break."

Bryle nods. It is not his way to waste time on useless debate. As he sees it, he has only one choice. Without weapons he is unlikely to win a fight against the sorcerer. In the maze there *are* such tools, and his choices may expand. Reaching inside his tunic, he starts to remove the tortoise that nestles there. This cavern has food and water for it. But some impulse stops him and he does not question. Without another word, he strides toward the doorway into the wizard's maze.

4

While the cave by which he'd entered the mountain, and the grotto he'd just left, were parts of a natural system, the maze itself is not. The first corridor he enters is rounded smooth, with a floor of stone flagging. Torches burn on the walls. Fifty paces in, the corridor ends abruptly at a pool of green water from which occasional bubbles rise. Faintly, he smells sulfur.

Bryle squats and thrusts his fingers into the pool. The water is cool but not cold. He sits on the edge and removes his boots. At his waist are tied two leather bags. The larger is his water skin. The smaller contains a few bites of jerky and a flint and tinder for campfires. He removes both bags, then takes the tortoise from his vest and stuffs it into the smaller one with the jerky.

Leaving boots and bags on the side of the pool, Bryle draws a few deep breathes, then pushes off into the water and dives. Torchlight filters downward so he can see. Three openings dot the wall across from him. A few strokes bring him close enough to feel warm water rushing from the one on the right.

Having verified the tunnel he wants, and that there is enough light to orient him, he returns to the surface and begins to feed his lungs with large gulps of air. He plucks up the bag with the tortoise in it and ties off the neck as tightly as possible, knowing it won't be completely waterproof but hoping it won't have to be. Strapping that bag, his water skin, and his boots to his belt, he takes another deep breath and dives once more.

He heads straight into the tunnel from which the warm water flows. Almost immediately the light begins to fade around him. He powers forward, swimming rapidly. The water darkens further and he glances over his shoulder once to see the green light growing distant.

Then light is gone and he is in blackness. He considers turning back. If he goes much farther he won't have breath for such a return. He pushes on instead, reaching out with his hands between strokes to brush the invisible walls to either side.

The corridor does not curve but the darkness within it deepens and takes on texture, seems to come alive. Bryle doesn't fear it. He's known darkness before. If anything, it has been a friend to him.

The first urges to breathe strike. They will grow stronger. And it is too late now to turn back. He hasn't the air. For a moment he wonders if the sorcerer *wants* him to drown. The being could have lied about the tunnels, but could also have simply closed off the outside cavern before Bryle reached it and left him to perish in flames. He pushes on.

His chest burns. His cheeks swell with bad air and he releases a few bubbles. He is swimming strongly but knows he won't be able to keep it up much longer. Then he sees a greenish light ahead. He fears he's gotten disoriented and turned around. It doesn't matter. His breath is almost gone. He must reach a haven soon or die.

The light grows, but so does the urge to breathe. Bubbles explode out of him now. He can't contain them. The taste of water fills his mouth, and it is foul with minerals. His limbs start to thresh in panic but he fights himself back under control. With all his strength, he swims toward the promising green.

That light is suddenly above him. He surges toward it, reaching for life. His head breaks the surface and pent up poisons erupt from his lungs. He gasps. The sweet air comes.

He hangs in the water for a while, then pulls himself toward the stone lip of the pool and drags himself out onto the floor. Torches burn on the walls but he sees immediately that this is not the same portion of the maze he started from. This room is bigger and cluttered with objects, including three standing statues.

Remembering a certain bag at his belt, Bryle sits up and unties the thongs binding it. Some water has seeped in and he dumps it out, but the whole bag never filled and the tortoise inside is perfectly safe. If a bit damp.

Bryle laughs. "Looks like you had a better trip than I did."

He has just emptied his boots and slid them on when, from deeper in the maze, there comes a sound. It rises and swells to a booming echo that rattles his nerves. He recognizes the cry of a hunting beast when he hears it.

5

The cry reanimates Bryle. He bounces up and casts quickly about for a weapon. One lies near the doorway into the next chamber. That door is closed by iron spikes upon which pieces of human skeleton hang. Just on Bryle's side of the spikes is a longsword with a simple, cross-shaped hilt. He hefts it, finds it lighter and thinner than the blades he's used to. He can adjust for that.

Feeling better with steel in his hand, Bryle returns to the first of the three stone statues and rotates it to face directly away from the other two. He turns the others toward each other, and the instant the last one is in place the iron spikes blocking the exit doorway slip down into the floor and the skeleton rattles free.

Taking the opening of the gateway trap to be a good sign, Bryle heads deeper into the maze, his newly acquired sword ready. His way is lit by torches and he wonders who keeps them lit since the sorcerer no longer commands here.

Would the conjured demon need light? Would the guardian beast? He has no answers to these questions and casts them from his mind.

Now, as Bryle ventures along the corridor, two doors show before him, opening upon different paths to his left and right. He soon finds more such doors, more such paths. Like most barbarians, Bryle's memory is good, but he knows that soon he'll be hopelessly mired in this maze. He needs a way to identify tunnels he's traversed, and quickly hits upon a strategy.

Drawing a torch from its cresset, he extinguishes it and uses the blackened tip to mark each tunnel he takes. In this way he makes progress, even if it is only to eliminate dead ends.

Bryle passes an alcove in the wall of one tunnel and sees within it a brass bound chest of the type treasures are stored in—for those who have such riches to store. Jewels encrust the chest; the lock is silver. These alone are wealth to such as Bryle. But he shakes his head and passes on, suspecting a trap for the greedy.

A short time later, Bryle passes a second chest and stops. His hackles rise. For a moment he is sure this is the *same* chest. But there are none of his black marks on the walls and this box is open. The bright shine of gold and copper coins reflects within the lid. He inches forward for a better look, not daring to cross the border of the alcove itself. On top of the gleaming coins lies a skull with a sword-cut between the brow ridges.

Bryle backs up, makes a mark to indicate he has passed this way, and continues. More doorways, more marks. Every tunnel begins to look the same, whether he has passed through it or not. He turns a corner and spies another open treasure chest. Two skulls lie within this one.

Yet, he knows now it *is* the same chest, the same place. There's no black smudge on the wall by the alcove but he'd noted something distinctive about the floor when passing this way before. It was scratched, as if by the scouring of hobnail boots. That scratch is here now.

Bryle gazes around. The hilt of the sword is sweaty in his hand. He understands what is happening. Something is toying with him. It erases his marks, making sure he remains lost. There is only one chest, one treasure. The skulls have been added by that which follows him.

In anger, Bryle lifts his sword to hack through the chest. Then he sighs, lowers the blade. He sits with his back to the wall opposite the treasure and sips water as he contemplates his next action. The tortoise stirs in its bag, reminding him that he has a companion. He draws out the small beast and holds it up to his face.

"Any advice?" he asks.

The black eyes do not blink as the creature meets his gaze.

Placing the tortoise on the floor, Bryle leans back and closes his own eyes. When he opens them again, the tortoise is crawling quickly toward the alcove where the chest sits. Afraid the small thing will be harmed by what he is sure is a trapped treasure, Bryle grabs for it. Too late. It crosses the border separating the alcove from the corridor itself.

A trap is sprung, but not the expected kind. The chest slides to one side and the wall behind it opens, revealing a hidden corridor. A frown creases Bryle's face. A moment before, he'd imagined that whatever was following him was erasing his marks to keep him lost. Now he wonders, instead, if it were trying to keep him near the treasure so he might discover this hidden way. In either case, he doubts the guardian beast would show such intelligence.

The demon knows I'm here.

Shrugging, Bryle climbs to his feet. He returns the tortoise to its bag before stepping through into the secret corridor. This tunnel runs straight and true until it leads him out onto a ledge overlooking a large, open shaft that extends both below and above him.

There is no need here for torches. The ceiling blazes with light, though Bryle cannot reckon the source. The air is fresh, however, so there must be some opening to the outside.

When he looks down, Bryle sees dozens of stone bridges crisscrossing the shaft in a bewildering array. One leads to a small square building of pure white that nestles at the bottom of the shaft. From here, he cannot tell which bridge reaches that building, but he senses that this is the heart of the maze. And his destination.

6

To Bryle's left is a small walkway that links to one of the bridges. He moves toward it, then freezes as he hears an odd chuckling sound coming from below. A solid stone railing borders the ledge and Bryle glances over it to see the black furred beast spoken of by the sorcerer.

The maze's guardian is built like a jackal but is large as a tiger. Its body is hunched as it moves; the sickle shaped talons on its front paws scrape the stone of the very walkway Bryle had planned to descend. The beast senses him and stands up straight. Bryle recognizes two things. First, the creature is female. Second, its belly is swollen with a late-term pregnancy.

For a few breathes, the gazes of Bryle and the beast clash. The monster's eyes are purple and all aglitter. Its mouth opens upon rows of teeth that resemble shards of broken glass. A low, rumbling chuckle pours from its throat, though there is nothing of humor in this sound.

The beast charges. In an instant it will reach Bryle on the ledge. He does not wish to fight it here, where there is scarcely room to swing a sword. He turns, steps up on the railing of the ledge. A dozen feet below runs one of the stone bridges that cross this chasm. He leaps toward it, drops swiftly, lands in a crouch.

Powering to his feet, he suddenly sees his way through this newest piece of the wizard's puzzle. Throwing himself into a run, he takes five steps and leaps downward again to a second bridge, then almost immediately to a third, and a fourth. Thus he cuts through the Gordian knot of the maze.

In a dizzying few moments he reaches the base of the shaft and the small white building he seeks. A door waits within it. Glancing over a shoulder, Bryle sees that the beast has followed the trail he blazed and is just behind him. Still, he has time. He grabs the door's latch and tugs.

The portal is locked.

7

Bryle turns to face the maze's guardian as it charges on all fours upon him. The ruff stands up on its neck; its triangular ears are laid back. The mouth drips a crimson saliva. No longer does the beast chuckle. Now it roars, the sound hot and hungry.

Bryle does not wish to kill the thing but will not die for it. He leaps to one side as it rises again on its hind legs and swipes at him with one taloned paw. Bryle strikes back, his blade humming. Blade meets paw and steel shears flesh. The paw goes flying. Blood sprays the white wall beside the barbarian.

The wound does not stop the guardian. It swarms over him, its bulk knocking him flat. He lands on his back and the creature's distended mouth dips for the kill. But Bryle is very fast and gets his sword between them, thrusts upward. The sword slides beneath the down-sweeping muzzle, lances into the throat and out the back of the thing's neck in an explosion of gore.

The thing writhes, tries to force its way down the blade to take Bryle's life. He strains to hold it back, then brings up his booted feet and plants them in the beast's chest. He heaves upward and with a great effort flips it over his head. It lands hard, tearing the sword from his grasp.

Bryle twists onto his belly, pushes himself to his feet. The beast starts to rise as well; its throat pumps blood. Bryle reaches it before it can get its legs under it. It swipes at him with its missing paw, splatters him with warm red. Bryle grabs the sword that still dangles from its throat, twists the blade and drags it free. A flood of scarlet spills down the beast's chest and it collapses onto its side.

Raising the blade high, Bryle prepares a downward stroke to take the thing's head. He does not follow through. The beast is finished. Its eyes watch Bryle for a dozen heartbeats. Then the purple glitter in them fades.

Bryle sinks to his knees beside the dead. The beast gives a last shudder, and a gout of pinkish liquid bursts from its lower body. Bryle is startled. Amidst the liquid is a fully intact caul, and inside the caul something struggles. The beast has given birth.

Hardly thinking now, only reacting, Bryle lets the sword fall to the floor and grabs for the caul. His fingers sink in, tear back the tissue. The smell assaults him.

Amniotic fluid gushes over his hands. A baby appears. Not human. Hairless. It does not much resemble its mother except for claws on the tips of its hands that are soapy looking and still soft. The small creature is not breathing.

Bryle knows little about birthing babies but has heard that midwives clean and rub newborns to trigger breathing. He uses his hand to wipe the young beast's face and nostrils, then begins to massage its upper body with his thumbs. Soon, the tiny mouth opens on a faint mewling cry and the chest starts to rise and fall.

Sighing with relief, Bryle reaches for his sword. He slices quickly through the umbilical cord and a will-o'-the-wisp of blue light leaps along the blade. The resulting tingle of shock makes him smile, for among his people it means a bond has formed. Tying off the cord, he kneels quietly and holds the little beast. It throbs with life.

"What? By all the hells? Am I going to do with you now?" he asks himself.

8

Even though he came here to find it, the white building behind Bryle is forgotten for the moment. He recalls it all of a sudden when he hears a door open. Twisting about, he sees a figure come from the building. It is cloaked and hooded, but the face is revealed and is both beautiful and vaguely reptilian. Iridescent scales dust its face.

Bryle's heart speeds. *The sorcerer's demon.*

He lunges quickly upright, one fist clutching the hilt of his sword, the other arm holding the baby beast against his chest. But the cloaked figure lifts its arms and shows two remarkably human-shaped hands, palms up in a gesture of peace. The hands are long fingered and delicate, purplish along the back and pale, pale yellow in the palm.

"I am not your enemy," the demon says. Its voice is as delicate as its hands and sweet as snow and cream.

"And what about the sorcerer who conjured you?" Bryle asks.

A pout twists the demon's mouth. "Oh, indeed I am *his* enemy. And I know he sent you here." The strange being closes one hand, then flashes it open again to show a small crystal vial in which rests a round, marble-sized object. "He sent you for this."

Bryle studies the object within the vial. It resembles a polished stone but he can see that it's an eye. He looks back at the demon but says nothing.

"No trick," the demon says. "This is what you seek."

"All right."

"I'll trade the sorcerer's eye for the small creature you hold."

"I don't think so."

"The sorcerer will not let you leave the maze without the eye. Besides …" The demon chuckles. "You mistake me about the newborn. I mean it no harm. It is *my* child."

Bryle's eyes widen. "That seems unlikely," he says finally.

"And you find demons and sorcerers completely unremarkable?"

Bryle snorts. "I take your meaning."

"I can give you the sorcerer's eye because with my child I will be able to counter the wizardry of the mage. He thinks to destroy me but I will surprise him."

"And you won't hurt the …" Bryle looks down at the creature nestled in the crook of his left arm, "child?"

"No. Nor will I harm you. Your concern for a helpless one does you honor."

"You don't sound much like the demon the sorcerer described," Bryle says.

Laughter sweeps the strange being and it takes a while to recover. Finally, it manages to speak: "Again you mistake me. I am no angel."

Bryle shrugs. "Who is?"

Bryle steps toward the demon then, holds out the child. The being's lipless mouth smiles and it takes the infant, cradles it gently. Finally, it looks up and tosses Bryle the eye.

The youth catches it, turns to go.

"One more thing," the demon says.

Bryle looks back, waits.

"The tortoise you carry in the pouch at your belt. You must not allow the sorcerer to have it."

Bryle's hand drops to the pouch of which the demon speaks. He wonders how the being knows of the tortoise and almost asks. Then he shrugs, says only, "I wouldn't have done so anyway."

The demon nods and again Bryle turns away. When he glances back once more there is no sign of the creature, or of its offspring.

9

Bryle returns the way he came, and this time finds a new door that leads him to a bridge across the flooded chamber. He is grateful not to have to make that swim again.

When he strides into the grotto beyond, there is still light coming through the hole in the ceiling. But it is evening light and will not last long. The sorcerer sits in the same place as before and his head immediately turns so his empty eye sockets point like arrows in Bryle's direction. A wet smile fills out the gaunt mouth.

"Not dead after all," the sorcerer says.

Bryle takes a few further steps and tosses the crystal vial toward the being on the throne. A gnarled hand snatches it from the air, brings it closer to the sorcerer's face. He sniffs.

"Excellent, excellent!"

The sorcerer uses a sharpened thumbnail to pop the cap from the vial. He pours the contents into his hand, then reaches up and pushes the eyeball into one socket. He looks back at Bryle and the barbarian finds that he preferred the empty socket to the filled one. The new eye is filmed with a scarlet cataract that forms a skull.

"You've done well," the sorcerer says. "The demon will be stopped, the human race spared."

"Then I'll be on my way," Bryle replies.

The sorcerer nods, waves a hand. Bryle hears a distant rumbling and imagines it is the sound of the seal over the external door of the cave sliding back. He starts across the grotto.

"There is ... one more thing," the sorcerer says.

Bryle sighs, turns to face the being. "Isn't there always?"

"The reptile in the leather satchel at your waist. Leave it with me."

"Why?"

"A ... sacrifice is needed to return my eye to full power."

Bryle shakes his head. "I can't do that. The tortoise brings me luck."

"A sacrifice is needed," the sorcerer says. "Of one kind or another."

"I'm sure there's a roach somewhere in this cavern. Or a worm. Use that."

"You'd die for a turtle?"

"Not if I could help it."

"You can't."

"I guess we'll see."

Bryle's right hand holds his sword. With his left, he removes the bag containing the tortoise and loosens the bindings at the top. Then he squats, empties the small creature onto a patch of moss. If he dies, the tortoise will at least be free.

The sorcerer watches with amusement. "I did not imagine you such a fool."

"I imagined you such a bastard," Bryle replies.

The sorcerer smirks. His one eye begins to pulse with light. Bryle's muscles tense as he prepares to move.

The sorcerer's eye flashes and a ruby spear of fire leaps from it toward Bryle, crystallizing the very air as it comes. Bryle starts to throw himself to one side, knows he won't be quick enough. Then, from just beneath his feet, a blue bolt of lightning surges skyward. Every shadow in the grotto is annihilated. The sorcerer is brilliantly lit and the lance of flame from his eye is stilled, as raindrops appear to be stilled when lightning flashes.

"Kill him now," a voice whispers in Bryle's head, and he is not sure if it is his own voice or another. No matter. He listens.

The burning spear stabbing from the sorcerer's eye is still lengthening, but with agonizing slowness. Bryle dodges it easily, closes the gap between himself and the wizard in an instant. The mage sees him coming. His head starts to turn. But nowhere near fast enough.

Bryle strikes. His sword darts beneath the ruby beam, sinks through the wizard's breastbone into the heart. The sorcerer convulses. The light from his eye blinks out. As he slumps, the eye rolls free of its socket and clink, clinks from the throne to the ground.

The world returns to normal. Bryle hears a murmur of footsteps and looks to see the demon come into the grotto. It crosses to the tortoise and picks it up, then walks past Bryle to the sorcerer's throne. Pushing the dead body out of the way, it seats itself.

Bryle opens his mouth, closes it again. He can think of nothing to say. But it seems the demon is not so tongue tied.

"I may have neglected to mention that my child is something more than just a physical entity. When you helped birth it, a fragment of its essence took up residence in …" It holds up the tortoise to show Bryle. "Thus, it was able to pass the mage's defenses without being discovered. As soon as he tried to use sorcery against you, it was able to offer aid. He could not predict such a tactic. Most of your kind do not count the small creatures of this world."

"I never *discount* them," Bryle says. "I was small myself once. I've not forgotten."

"You are a rather unusual barbarian."

"Then you don't know many barbarians."

"Perhaps that is true."

"Are you free now? With the sorcerer's death?"

"I am."

"Should I fear for the world's destruction then? As the wizard claimed?"

The demon chuckles. "You should fear it. But not from me. Your own kind will be the cause."

"How long do we have?"

"A millennium. Give or take."

The faintest of smiles twists Bryle's lips. "Time for a few ales then," he says.

"A few."

Bryle nods and turns away. It is almost night in the grotto now and he knows he'll have to feel his way from this place. But the darkness will not balk him.

"Barbarian," the demon calls.

Bryle stops but does not look back.

"Follow the light," the demon whispers in a voice like a harp.

Bryle hears a susurration of movement. Then a pearly glow blooms behind him and slowly spreads across the grotto. He sees his direction. And he sees— cast upon the wall in front of him, the shadows of wings.

†

ABOUT THE AUTHOR

Charles Allen Gramlich
is the author of the Talera
fantasy trilogy, the thriller
Cold in the Light, and the
SF novel *Under the Ember
Star*. His stories have been
collected primarily in
three anthologies, *Bitter Steel*, (fantasy), *Midnight in Rosary*
(Vampires/Werewolves), and *In the Language of Scorpions*
(Horror). He is also the author of *Write With Fire*, a book
about writing and publishing. His works are available in print
and ebook at Amazon, Barnes & Noble, and Wildside Press.
Additionally, some of Charles's stories are available in
novella length packets or as standalone ebooks from
Amazon. These include *Killing Trail* (Westerns), *Harmland*
(Noir/Horror), *MicroWeird* (Flash Fiction), and Harvest of
War (*Fantasy*).

Charles lives with his wife in Louisiana. He blogs at
http://charlesgramlich.blogspot.com/.

Also by Charles Allen Gramlich

Novels

Cold in the Light, Invisible College Press, 2002
Swords of Talera, Borgo Press, 2007.
Wings Over Talera, Borgo Press, 2007.
Witch of Talera, Borgo Press, 2007.
Under the Ember Star, Borgo Press, 2012. (Wildside
    Double #25)

Chapbooks

Wanting the Mouth of a Lover, Spec House of Poetry,
    2008.

Single author collections from Borgo Press:

Bitter Steel: Tales and Poems of Epic Fantasy, 2010.
*Midnight in Rosary: Tales of Vampires and
    Werewolves in Crimson and Black*, 2011.
*In the Language of Scorpions: Tales of Horror from
    the Inner Dark*, 2012.

ABOUT THE VERIDICAL DREAMS SERIES

The Veridical Dreams series began in memory of Kyle J. Knapp, poet and writer who passed away in a house fire in 2013 at the age of twenty-three. His dream journals served as the inspiration for a collection of short stories fleshed out from fragments of these sleep derived mind trips, which became *The Lizard's Ardent Uniform and Other Stories* as volume one of the series.

An offshoot sprang from that first volume of Veridical Dreams in the form of The Kyler Knightly and Damon Cole series. This line features two time-traveling agents who police and protect the chronosphere, in four short adventures written by Garnett Elliott: "The Zygma Gambit," "Carnosaur Weekend," "Babylon Heist," and "Apocalypse Soon."

The Veridical Dreams series continues with additional offerings in single shots with "Treasure of Ice and Fire" by Wayne D. Dundee and now "Mage, Maze, Demon" by Charles Allen Gramlich.

MORE FROM THE **VERIDICAL DREAMS** SERIES

THE LIZARD'S ARDENT UNIFORM & Other Stories — (Veridical Dreams Vol. I) takes you on several voyages into everyday nightmares, bizarre detours, and hellish worlds through seven stirring tales of crime, science fiction, literary, and fantasy, inspired from thought-provoking fragments from the dream journals of Kyle J. Knapp, writer and poet who passed away in 2013 at the age of twenty-three.

TREASURE OF ICE AND FIRE — From the Valley of Gahm in the land of Brassik, a rogue priest named Nindocai hears the transcendent ringing of a mythical mallet--a call for action from the Goddess Arya. Leading a rag-tag band over frigid, snow-packed terrain, Nindocai goes in search of the hammer of the gods that can free his people, or in the wrong hands could spell annihilation for mankind. But they may not complete their quest with the tyrannical Wyvar regulators, that rule the land with an iron fist, out to destroy Nindocai and his followers at any cost. What emanates from deep within the ruins of a secret underground chamber ... does great wealth await, or is death beyond the cavern's mouth?

    Best-selling author Wayne D. Dundee, known as one of the modern architects of hardboiled fiction, directs his prose skills toward crafting a fantasy tale that rivals the classics of the genre.

BONUS STORY
FROM VOLUME I OF THE **VERIDICAL DREAMS** SERIES

THE LIZARD'S ARDENT UNIFORM

Chris F. Holm

Kyle Williams was sleeping. He was sleeping, and this was just a dream. There was no monster in his backyard.

At least, that's what he told himself—although his eyes told him something else entirely.

His alarm clock glowed 3:17. Kyle's mother had put him to bed nearly seven hours ago. He'd been sleeping soundly until a few minutes back, when he was roused by a short, sharp rap that echoed through the night, and a subsequent lessening of the darkness all around him.

Light, faint and white like the moon's, spilled in through his bedroom window.

But tonight, Kyle knew, the moon was new. It said so on the astronomical calendar that hung above his desk. That calendar, along with his very own reflector telescope, was gift from his father—or, more accurately, a bribe—given to him shortly after they left Boston for Santa Fe.

Kyle's father had been a tenure-track professor of physics at MIT when Ardent Industries came calling, and Kyle himself had been happily ensconced in third grade at The Bellwether Academy, which he'd attended since pre-K. He wasn't present for the phone call, but he remembered afterward listening in on his parents' conversation from the upstairs landing of their Beacon Hill row house, his right cheek pressed against the balusters as he strained to hear.

"Are you sure you want to do this, Eric? Leave MIT? Uproot Kyle?"

"For the chance to have the lab of my dreams, and all the funds I'd ever need to continue my research? For the chance to prove to the world that limitless clean energy is not only theoretically possible, but attainable in our lifetime? Allie, how could I possibly turn that down?"

Apparently, he couldn't, because soon after, they packed their things and drove the family Volvo to their new home—a sprawling ranch-style house on the outskirts of Santa Fe, with russet-colored desert all around. Ardent paid to have their belongings shipped ahead of them, so when they arrived, their furniture was already set up—their dark-stained Colonial pieces looking awkward and out-of-place in this rustic, Southwestern setting. Kyle had barely spoken in the four days it took them to make the drive. He was too heartsick. He missed his old school, his old house, his old life. But when he walked into his bedroom to find amidst his old belongings, a brand new Celestron NexStar SLT Series 130 SLT telescope, his foul mood evaporated.

"I thought you might enjoy that," said his father from his doorjamb with a grin. "You'll see a lot more stars here than you ever could in Boston. Too much light pollution there to make them out, even on a clear night. But way out here, who knows what you might see?"

His father was right. In his whole life, Kyle had never seen so many stars as he had that first night. And thanks to his telescope, he soon found there was more to the night sky than he'd ever imagined. The pock-marked surface of the moon. The reddish haze of the Orion Nebula. The majesty of Saturn's rings. The monster in his backyard.

When that unearthly glow shone through his bedroom window and cast long shadows of his telescope on its tripod, he slipped out of bed and padded, barefoot and pajama-clad, over to the window for a look. What he saw was a beam of light shining down upon a figure in the darkness, some thousand feet of scrub-strewn desert away. At this distance, Kyle could make out nothing of the man—for at that point, he still assumed it was a man—so he aimed his scope in his direction. All he got for his trouble was a blurry mess. But when he dialed back the magnification and adjusted the focus, a figure resolved, standing in an undulating column of white. And that figure was not human.

It *was* human-sized, at least. Somewhere between five-five and six feet, Kyle guessed, although it stood in a strange, feral half-crouch, which made its full height hard to estimate. It had two arms, two legs, and a head, each in the usual place. But its skin—every inch of which was visible, on account of the creature was naked—was plated with thick, green scales like a lizard's. Its hands and feet, while broadly humanoid, terminated in nasty looking claws that glinted like onyx in the strange, pulsing light and seemed capable of retracting at will, because they twitched as if testing the air around the beast, and the ground beneath its feet. Its head, which was tilted to the heavens as though basking in the light's glow, put Kyle in mind of a boa constrictor. Its eyes glistened like puddles of black ink, occasionally clouding over for a moment when the creature blinked—translucent nictitating membranes sliding across its eyes like an eclipse viewed on fast-forward.

When Kyle looked into those eyes, he had a sudden, panicked thought the creature could see him, and he hit the floor. But when his galloping heart slowed to a trot and he screwed up the courage to peek through the eyepiece once more, he realized the lizard-beast hadn't moved: it was still staring up at the unseen light-source high above. Kyle wondered what could possibly generate so bright a beam. He followed the beam upward with his telescope until it dwindled to no more than a single strand of spider-silk bisecting the crushed velvet of the night sky, but he saw no source. He increased the magnification, and the beam widened.

Using that method—an upward tilt until the beam dwindled down to nothing followed by an increase in magnification—he followed the light back to its source, a spinning disc of deeper dark against the starry black. And as he zoomed in upon the aperture from whence the undulating beam sprang, his reflector scope amplifying the light's intensity, a strange sensation overtook Kyle. It began as a hum deep inside his inner ear, a rattle in his molars. And then, at once, he heard them.

No. *Heard* wasn't quite right. It was more like he and they—the creature on the ground, and the one with whom it was conversing on the ship—occupied the same headspace. Ideas flew back and forth between them in a rush, all filtered through the limited experience of Kyle's eight-year-old mind.

From the ship, an interrogative barrage of images. A four-star general, his face unseen, his chest spangled with multicolored medals. A discarded pair of coveralls, plucked off the floor. A policewoman adjusting her belt and putting on her hat.

Did you acquire the uniform?

The beast below's reply registered in Kyle's mind as a box checked on a to-do list, a big thumbs-up, a finish line proudly crossed.

Yes.

The ship, its tone somehow once more questioning: A hand bashing through glass marked IN CASE OF EMERGENCY and retrieving a fire-ax. A cartoon burglar wearing a raccoon-like mask over his eyes and tiptoeing through the darkness, a bag slung over his shoulder. A light bulb glowing ever brighter, and then bursting. Steam billowing from the cooling towers of a nuclear power plant.

What about the … and here, Kyle's mind struggled to grasp the creature's meaning. It was somewhere between *power source* and *weapon* in his mind. But before he could reconcile the images his brain had been bombarded with, the creature on the ground replied; his mother's kitchen timer approaching zero, a clock just seconds from striking midnight.

Soon.

Then, suddenly, the tone changed. The light grew … agitated somehow. Angry. Kyle's mind flooded with red-tinted images of an ear pressed against a wall, a TV cop wearing a wire.

They knew someone was listening.

The light blinked out, plunging Kyle into night's full dark. Kyle hit the deck, knocking over his telescope in his haste. A cold sweat broke out across his back and neck. He lay there in the darkness trembling for what seemed like forever.

Helpless. Exposed. Vulnerable.

Eventually, his fear of staying put overwhelmed his fear of moving. He belly-crawled from his spot beneath the window back to his bed, and then—gathering his courage—leapt off the floor, tossing his blankets high into the air. He landed in the boy-sized divot at the center of his mattress as they settled over him.

Kyle lay that way for hours, his fear of the lizard-beast bursting in to find him balanced somewhat by a child's faith in the mystical protection afforded by pulling the covers over one's head.

And then, as the coming sun painted orange the eastern horizon, he slept.

* * *

Kyle tossed and turned well into morning, trying in vain to catch up on the sleep the monster in his yard had stolen from him. He ignored his mother's 8 a.m. urgings to get up, and her attempts to bribe him with chocolate chip pancakes at ten. But it was no use; sleep was fleeting, and when it came, so too did nightmare visions of lizard-beasts hunting for him in the darkness—of spotlights zigzagging across the desert floor as half-seen ships above searched high and low. So instead, he lay beneath the covers, queasy from hunger and exhaustion both, but too frightened to come out.

"I'm worried about him, Eric," said his mother from just outside his door, shortly after her failed pancake bribe. "He's been in bed all morning, and refuses to come out."

"Maybe he's sick."

"He's not, as far as I can tell. His forehead felt normal, and he doesn't sound congested. I think he's … frightened?"

"Probably just had a nightmare."

"Some nightmare. Will you talk to him?"

A long pause. A sigh. And then Kyle's dad said, "If it'll make you feel better, sure."

Kyle heard, but did not see, the door open. Felt the mattress rock beneath the sudden weight of his father, as he sat down on the edge of the bed.

"Hey, kiddo, you okay?"

Kyle nodded beneath the blankets.

"You know I'd find that more convincing if you'd come out of there."

Reluctantly, Kyle poked his head free.

"Rough night?"

Kyle nodded again.

"Bad dreams?"

"I guess."

"You guess?"

Kyle shrugged. "Seemed pretty real to me."

"You want to talk about it, maybe?"

Kyle shook his head.

"Sometimes talking through a bad dream helps you feel better. You realize how silly it sounds when you say it out loud, and it stops being scary."

He waited, but Kyle said nothing. "Okay," he said, "I won't make you. But your mom's pretty worried about you. You think you could maybe come out and get some breakfast so she knows you're okay?"

"I suppose," Kyle said.

"Attaboy," his dad said, tousling Kyle's hair. "C'mon. I hear tell she's making pancakes."

The two of them walked hand-in-hand down the hall to the kitchen. Right before they entered the room, Kyle's dad exclaimed, "Look what I found!"

For a moment, Kyle had the irrational fear that his kitchen would be full of angry lizard-monsters, all slavering at the chance to sink their teeth into his tender flesh. But when they rounded the corner, there was no one in the kitchen but Kyle's mother. She was mixing up a bowl of pancake batter, and she beamed when she caught sight of him. "Hey, sleepy-head," she said. "You hungry?"

Kyle nodded.

"Good," she said, flicking on the stovetop to heat the skillet. "What about you?" she asked her husband.

"Starving," he said, "but I've got to stop into the lab. In fact," he said, looking at his watch, "I should have been there twenty minutes ago."

"You have to eat," she said.

"I know," he replied. "But I'm already late, and you haven't even started cooking yet."

"Promise you'll grab something on the way?"

"I promise."

Kyle watched his dad lean in and give his mom a peck on the cheek. Watched her fingers graze his chest as he pulled away, a simple gesture of affection. Suddenly, the horrid images of last night that plagued him well into this morning seemed a world away: a bad dream fading into distant memory.

"Later, kiddo," said his dad as he pushed open the screen door and stepped outside.

"Later, Dad!" Kyle called back, smiling.

But as the screen door's old spring yanked it closed, and its wooden frame clacked against the jamb, Kyle's blood ran cold. Because he knew at once that was the short, sharp rap that roused him late last night. That had brought him to the window in the first place.

What did it mean? Had that monster tried to get into the house? He didn't know, but he was sure now what he'd seen hadn't been a dream. Which meant they weren't safe here. Which meant he had to tell someone.

He looked to his mom, but she was busy cooking pancakes, and wasn't paying him any mind. *Not that she'd believe me anyways*, he thought.

But Dad might.

Kyle ran to the screen door. Tried to call out to his dad. But the words died on his lips, and all that came out was a strangled wheeze.

Because as he reached the door, he saw his dad crouched in the driveway like a feral animal, his head tracking slowly from left to right. Kyle followed his dad's gaze, and soon spotted the object that had attracted his attention: a dun brown deer mouse, scurrying across their cracked dirt drive.

As its path across the driveway brought it near to Kyle's dad, his father leapt quick as death, and came up with the squirming rodent in his hands. Then he snapped its neck, and the poor mouse squirmed no more.

And as Kyle watched, he tilted his head back, opened his mouth wide—revealing a second mouth inside it brimming with sharp glinting teeth, like a snake's—and lowered the dead mouse into it by its tail.

Then the thing wearing Kyle's dad climbed into the family Volvo and took off for Ardent Industries, the dirt kicked up by the tires hanging heavy in the air.

†

BONUS STORY
FROM APOCALYPSE SOON

BABYLON HEIST

Garnett Elliott

Outside a Bronze Age sun baked the mud bricks of a thousand dwellings, beat down on the heads of slaves, soldiers, and nobles alike, dulled the bray of the onagers and parched the myriad voices of the marketplace, even hoarsened the Priest King himself, as he called out noon rites from the tallest ziggurat in the city.

But there were places the sun couldn't reach …

Beneath an abandoned temple near the hovels of Buzzard Gate, a secret chamber had been dug. Light from a clay lamp flickered in the cooling darkness. It threw shadows across the faces of three men and one woman, hunched around a table of precious cedar wood. They spoke in whispers and passed a jar brimming with black beer.

Criminals, all.

"Let me express my gratitude," said the oldest, a merchant-type with silver shekel weights woven into his white beard. "First for your being so prompt in response to my summons. Second, for having the bravery to—"

The man-mountain of a Sumerian sitting to his right let out a grunt. "Time is money. Spare us the pleasantries, Arshan, and get down to the job."

"Shumir doesn't speak for me," said the plump, painted woman seated to the old man's left. A fillet of tiny golden bells circled her brow. She wore a harness of crisscrossed threads hung with hundreds more, and there was a tinkling sound as she passed the beer. "Some of us have plenty of time."

"Ha." Shumir leveled a thick finger. "That's because your 'Temple of Holy Love' doesn't open for business until nightfall. What's a glorified whore doing here, anyway?"

Arshan cleared his throat. "I'll remind you that Iltani is a priestess. As such, she plays as vital role in our plans."

"So you keep saying." Shumir nodded at the fourth member of the group, who had yet to speak. "And what about *him*? What do we need some blonde Hellene for? 'Kyros the Eel.' I've never heard of him."

Faces swiveled to regard the foreigner.

"Well, Kyros," said Arshan, "would you like to give us an accounting of yourself?"

The slender man drew a deep breath. He'd been dreading introductions all morning. And not because he was supposedly a Macedonian Greek, who'd left his hilly homeland for the gold and intrigue of Babylon. No, Kyros the Eel, aka Kyler Knightly, field agent for Continuity Inc., had traveled back in time more than three thousand years to get a piece of this action.

"I'd, ah, like more beer, please."

* * *

Calling the stuff "beer" was too charitable. Flat, warm, and floating with hazy chunks, you didn't drink the dark liquid so much as chew it. But alcohol was alcohol. Kyler drained the jar, stealing a glance over the rim at his companions. Like him, one of them wasn't who they appeared to be. Another time-traveler, sent back to swipe a priceless artifact for a collector in the twenty-third century. Continuity Inc. had received solid intel *what* they were after, but not *who* was involved. Finding out was Kyler's job. He'd spent several days nosing around the Babylonian underworld before he'd discovered this group. The fact they were planning something big, and soon, he took as more than a coincidence.

"The man's dry," Iltani said, noting the empty jar with a smile. She clapped her hands. "Slave! More beer."

A tall Egyptian eunuch appeared, veiled like a woman. He hustled over another jar and placed it on the table before scurrying off.

Kyler reached for the brew. Irritated with his silence, Arshan said: "Our Greek friend specializes in getting inside tight places. Hence the nickname."

"Bah." Shumir spat. "Unnecessary. With my muscles I can bore through any mud-brick wall."

"Your muscles are part of the problem," Arshan said. "Cutting a hole to fit those shoulders would take too long. And timing is crucial if we want to break into the manor of Naram Eil."

Iltani straightened. "So old Naram's our mark. What's the loot?"

Arshan and Shumir traded looks. "A tablet," the white-bearded man said at last. "A treatise on astronomy Naram keeps in his library. There's an Assyrian scholar willing to pay fifty gold minas for it—and I can probably drive him higher."

Iltani's painted face went pale. "*Fifty* gold minas …"

"I wouldn't bother putting a caper together for less," Arshan said.

The linguistic chip implanted in Kyler's mastoid process was having a hard time with Neo-Babylonian slang; words like "mark," "loot," and "caper" were criminal argot, and not in the regular lexicon. So he was several seconds behind the conversation. But he was willing to bet the "Assyrian scholar" offering the money was several thousand years in the future. And the piece of clay they were talking about was none other than the Kidinnu Tablet, a significant work of early science.

"Enough," Shumir said, looking like he wanted to spit again. He rounded on Arshan. "Whatever's going down, one thing's for certain: your fingers won't touch any of the dirty work. Not our Honest Arshan. So tell us the master plan, already."

If the old man took any offense, he didn't show it. "The plan," he said, unrolling a hide map across the table. "Now, that *is* a thing of beauty ..."

* * *

After the meeting, Kyler slipped off to a shadowy bar to guzzle date wine. His nerves were still shot. Everyone he glimpsed, from the one-armed bartender to the withered old scribe sitting two stools down might be a spy for Arshan. Or Shumir. Or Iltani. They could have someone tailing him right now.

He reached down to touch the focus object he carried at his side. A bronze-headed mace, "borrowed" from the British Museum and contemporaneous with this time period. The artifact had allowed Continuity Inc.'s powerful Zygma projector to send him back circa 770 B.C. He took a measure of comfort knowing he could also use it to bash in someone's head.

"Hot day, isn't it?" the bartender said, giving him a look that could mean suspicion or nothing at all.

"It is at that."

He paid with a silver shaving and got the hell out of there. 'Hell' being an apt choice of words. The temperature in the offal-strewn streets hovered around a hundred and twenty Fahrenheit. No breeze stirred. Babylon's massive walls blocked most of the wind from the plain, and the ubiquitous mud brick trapped heat like a sponge. To make the vision complete, a huge tower straight out of Bruegel dominated the skyline, with antlike figures ascending a ramp around the exterior.

He passed a squad of soldiers in long leather capes. War season was coming up fast, and there was talk of conflict with Nineveh. He shook his head. Things never changed, did they?

A quarter-mile from Buzzard's Gate lay a smaller portal called Whore's Gate, leading to an older residential section. Kyler slunk down the adjacent alley, ready to pull his mace on any would-be muggers. He brushed aside a pile of desiccated straw to reveal a crack in the wall. A tiny roll of parchment jutted out from it.

He unrolled the message, written in Continuity Inc. cipher. Translated, it read:

NOTHING NEW ON MY END. MISS AIR CONDITIONING AND BUBBLES IN BEER. WILL RENDEVOUSZ AT THE USUAL PLACE.

Kyler's uncle Damon had been sent back under-cover as well. Communicating with him by shortwave was strictly a no-no, given that another time traveler might have a receiver. He took a stylus from his tunic and clicked out a hidden ballpoint.

IT'S GOING DOWN TONIGHT.

Message replaced, he hurried back the way he came.

* * *

"*Cops*. Into the shadows, moron."

Shumir grabbed Kyler by the arm and hauled him flat against a wall. A chariot drawn by four onagers rattled close. The soldier at the reins gripped a three-meter spear, and the scarred man crouched beside him, dressed in a corselet of bronze scales, held a compound bow. Their eyes raked the street. But the moon was a mere sliver, and the absence of lamps made Babylonian night dark as a closet. The chariot passed without slowing.

"Keep bungling," Shumir whispered, "and I'll drag your ass back to Arshan, tablet or no tablet."

"Sorry."

"Not as sorry as we'll both be if we're caught. This is the wealthy quarter, and crimes against nobility mean death."

They'd had to slink through several gates, past checkpoints and guard posts to get here. The richer portion of Babylon felt like a different city. Brick surfaces had been enameled in vibrant reds, yellows, and blues. Walls enclosed gardens of slender date palms, where unseen fountains splashed. Even the air smelled better; human waste was carted off to be dumped elsewhere. Night-blooming jasmine replaced the stink of open sewage.

They stole across a broad plaza. Shumir carried an ox-hide bag that occasionally made a clinking noise. "There's our target," he said, nodding at a walled manor nearby. "Naram Eil's place."

Kyler recalled the layout from Arshan's map. The estate boasted a tall tower, rising well above the surrounding four-meter wall. Lamplight flickered steadily at the top. Among other things, Naram Eil was an amateur astronomer.

Shumir's grin showed white against his soot-blackened face. "Stargazing as usual. Lucky for us he's got his head pointed at the sky, and not the grounds below."

They found a shadowed spot well away from any street traffic. In lieu of checking his watch, Kyler gauged the time from the moon's position. Close to midnight.

The tinkle of bells carried up the plaza. After a tense minute Kyler could make out their source; a half-dozen feminine shapes, approaching on bare feet. They'd painted their faces with talc and kohl, nude save for the jangling harnesses they wore. Iltani marched at their head. The temple prostitutes made straight for the manor's front gate. Iltani clashed a pair of cymbals together and waited, her face expectant.

"There's our distraction," Shumir said. "Move."

Kyler approached the manor wall. Gritting his teeth, he knelt on all fours and made a human table. Shumir planted a foot on his back. For a second, unbearable weight pressed against his spine. Then Shumir leapt up and caught the top of the wall. With barely a grunt, he hauled himself up one-handed. Fucking showoff. He hooked a leg over the far side and dangled his muscled arm towards Kyler. A jump, and Kyler grabbed him by the wrist. With a combination of Shumir's strength and his own scrabbling, he gained the top.

The wall was half a meter thick. Kyler pivoted on his knees to get a view of the courtyard. Young ash trees formed a walkway around a low fountain, filled with shimmering water. Just beyond he could see the inward side of the front gate and four hairy silhouettes hunkered around it. Those would be the Guti tribesmen old Naram employed as guards. They were talking in gruff voices through a small window to Iltani, on the other side. Negotiating prices.

Shumir huffed. "I guess Arshan was right about her being useful. I wouldn't care to take my chances with that lot."

Kyler nodded at the shadowed main house. "We don't have much time."

They leapt down among ferns and flowers. Shumir's bag made a muffled clank that thankfully didn't carry far. "Around back," he whispered. "Trying to force the front door puts us in view of the guards."

They circled to the rear of the house. There were no windows on the ground level, and the slits above were too narrow for even Kyler's thin frame. Ergo, they had to bore through the wall. Shumir felt along the bricks with an artist's concentration. He halted, nodding to himself, and pulled a strange tool from his bag. It had a wooden disk at one end and an auger-shaped head.

Without explanation, he thrust the bit into the wall. A turn of the disk, and the primitive drill started tearing away chunks of mud brick.

Kyler watched him work in silence, straining his ears for the sound of any approaching Guti. "This is taking too long," he whispered.

"Like hell it is. Look, I'm already through."

He pulled the drill out to reveal a small hole. From the bag he took a curved bronze rod that looked like a crowbar, and inserted it into the opening. A heave, and he levered out a brick. Someone with lesser strength would've had a harder time, but Shumir took only minutes to make a Kyler-sized opening.

"In you go," he said. "The working girls' business won't last long, so get that tablet and get out. I'll be waiting in the corner over there, behind the bush."

Leaving the hard part to me, Kyler thought. He wriggled into the jagged hole. His mace threatened to snag on a brick, but by turning his hip he managed to worm through.

Murky darkness on the other side. His palms and knees touched a floor of cool stone, smooth as marble. After a few seconds his eyes adjusted. Lamplight guttered from somewhere ahead. He crawled for it, striving to remember the layout from Arshan's map. The library was on the ground floor. A confirmed bachelor, Naram Eil kept no women. With him up in his tower and the servants asleep, the lower rooms should be vacant. That was the theory, at least.

He found a clay lamp in the foyer. Steps of polished basalt led upwards, but he skirted those, taking the lamp with him as he headed towards a hallway. The house was tomb-silent. He became too aware of his own breathing, the echo of his footfalls. If caught, he'd be punished in the most literal manner possible: his dead body would be used to shore up the hole Shumir had made. "Eye for an eye, tooth for a tooth," came directly from Hammurabi's law code, enacted in Babylon one thousand years earlier.

But there was more at stake here than his own safety. He swallowed fear and crept down the hall. At the far end, a doorway opened onto a chamber with niches carved into the walls. Clay tablets lay stacked within.

Jackpot.

Conscious of time draining away, he played lamplight over the library's shelves. There were at least a hundred tablets, all crowded with wedge-shaped cuneiform. Not a large selection by modern standards, but enough to take too long if he wasn't careful. Luckily, he had an excellent reference hidden in his homespun tunic. A copy of the Kidinnu Tablet, exact as they could make it in the twenty-third century, after sections had crumbled away. Using the copy as a guide, he shuffled through tablets until he found a match. The real one went into his tunic along with the fake. Ironic, but the best way to protect it for now was to keep it close. Arshan and crew would receive the copy. Kyler would then return the tablet to Naram Eil, after he'd nabbed his time-traveling thief.

Satisfied, he turned to the doorway. And froze.

A sleek black leopard had come padding into the room. The beast sat on its haunches, observing him with lambent yellow eyes. A silver collar encircled its thick neck.

Kyler silently cursed. Arshan's plans hadn't allowed for pets.

The leopard let out a growl. It might be playful, or it might be a prelude to ripping his guts open. He considered the mace at his side, but he didn't really want to brain the beautiful animal. Also, killing this far back in time was frowned on; even the loss of a big cat could snowball into unforeseen consequences.

The leopard got up and slunk over. It nuzzled his hand before growling again, louder this time. Slow as he could, Kyler withdrew the stylus he'd used in the alley. Two strong clicks. Instead of a ballpoint, an eight gauge hypodermic slid from the tip.

The cat's growl edged into a roar. Black lips pulled back over bared incisors. He plunged the needle into its neck. The stylus hissed, injecting a full reservoir of toxin. Paralytics designed for a ninety-kilogram man made the leopard's muscles spasm. It went rigid before keeling over.

Kyler's heart started to pound. Could someone have heard all that growling? He left the lamp where he'd set it down and hurried from the library. Passing the foyer, he glimpsed a stooped figure coming around a corner at the top of the stairs. He dove for the smooth-floored chamber. A short distance away gaped the hole Shumir had made. He ploughed through without getting stuck.

Out into the gardens. Compared to the house's dark interior, it seemed almost bright. But where was Shumir? He searched the shadowed corner where he'd said he'd be waiting. No trace.

Rustling noises. A pair of broad-shouldered shapes came loping down the side of the house. Their interlude with Iltani's 'maidens' must be over. Kyler pressed himself against the ground.

An old man's voice cried out from the front of the house. The guards wheeled and started running in that direction. Naram must've already found the leopard. They'd search the house, find the hole, and find *him*, a short distance away.

He leapt for the wall's rim, but couldn't reach it. Goddamn Shumir. He must've known he would've left him trapped here—

Wait a second. How would Shumir have gotten out? He wasn't any taller.

Kyler felt along the wall. His fingers brushed a deep gouge in the brick, at the perfect height for a foothold. Shumir could've made it with one of his tools. He thrust his toes inside, pushed, and scrambled over the top of the wall. Hang-dropped to the other side.

The open plaza stretched around him. Instead of feeling relief, the back of his neck prickled. He sensed eyes watching from the darkness.

Kyler had been a Level Two Precognitive before becoming a field agent. His intuitions had a habit of turning into solid facts. And right now, his intuition screamed to leap for cover.

He did so. Two meters to his left a public fountain bubbled, and he hurled himself behind it.

His retinas flashed. A finger of ruby-red sparks angled down to touch the space he'd just vacated. It scorched a pattern on the paving stones and followed to where he crouched. There was a *whoosh* as the fountain's water converted to steam.

Someone had brought a laser to ancient Babylon. He rolled and popped his head up. Again, the ruby light flashed, and he ducked. This time the whooshing went on for a long moment, as the gunner raked the fountain. Either excited or frustrated. Steam rose in a large, roiling cloud.

Kyler stood up. When the beam flashed again it struck the cloud and diffracted into a harmless spray of color. Smoke would've been more effective, but what the hell. He traced the laser's path to a wall top some thirty meters away.

The beam winked out. Likely, the capacitor needed several seconds to charge again.

Likely.

But if he stayed here, pinned, his sniper would find another angle.

Expecting to be fried at any moment, he broke from the fountain and ran.

* * *

Twice Kyler got lost bolting down darkened side-streets and alleys. Twice he had to retrace his steps. Soldiers, cesspools, and staggering drunks seemed to materialize out of the warm night air. He eluded them all.

The twisting streets began to look familiar. Another few blocks and he found his safe house; a bottom floor room in a four-story tenement. He had to wake the landlord by pounding on the door, which got him a sharp look, but thankfully, no questions. His room was a tiny cubicle with a straw tick and the Babylonian equivalent of a chamber pot. A slit-window let in air. During the day, the place was an oven.

He rolled up the tick and placed the tablet—the real one—in a niche he'd dug the day before. Hopefully, Damon would have access to a better hiding place. Loot secured, he collapsed into a corner and allowed himself the luxury of several deep breaths.

Safe. For now, anyways. Nothing like a leopard or a laser-potting sniper to remind of one's mortality. He fought the urge to reach under his tunic and activate the recall beacon clipped there. A quantum-entangled signal could haul him back to the present in minutes.

But that would mean leaving Uncle Damon high and dry. And there was still the matter of the mystery-thief.

Though he had a damn good idea who it was.

* * *

Babylon came to life in the ash-colored dawn. The sun had risen early for another day of merciless scorching, throwing shadows across the abandoned temple. As Kyler approached, he could hear the echoes of stalls being erected in the market near Buzzard Gate. Commerce never waited long.

He crept into the temple courtyard, eyes wary. Arshan's plan called for a regroup the morning after the heist, to exchange the tablet. It had struck Kyler as the perfect opportunity for a double-cross.

But some of his tension eased when he spied Shumir waiting in plain sight. The big man leaned against a cracked stone altar, his arms folded. He grinned at Kyler. "Glad to see you made it."

"No thanks to you."

"Hey now, don't get hostile." Shumir was keeping his right hand tucked behind his back. "Sorry I had to ditch you in the garden, but those tribesmen were loose."

"Where's Arshan?"

"Not here yet. You got the tablet, right?"

"You going to try and laser me for it again?"

To his credit, Shumir's face remained calm. "I don't know what you're talking about."

"Sure you don't. Two things you need to know, pal. One, I've hidden the tablet in a secure place. Two, I didn't come back in time alone. My uncle Damon's armed and watching us right now."

That last part was a bluff, but it sounded good.

"Alright," Shumir said in Anglic, stretching to show the auto-pistol in his right hand. "How'd you figure it?"

"Your muscles. They don't have deltoid grafting in the ancient Middle East. Another thing; minus the extra pigment and the hook someone added to your nose, you look just like a professional wrestler from a couple years back. Big Hoss McAdams, I think his name was."

"Big *Boss* McAdams. But close enough."

"One thing I don't get. If you brought a laser back, why bother with all the subtleties? You could've roasted Naram's guards from the wall, and burned through his front door."

McAdams shook his head. "That would blow my cover to any other time travelers. No, I had to take a low-tech approach."

"Until you tried to shoot me, anyway."

"Nothing personal."

Kyler felt his hands clench. "You've got no idea what you're doing. The Kidinnu Tablet's a big chunk of early science. Steal it, and we could be travelling back to a radically different future."

"Bullshit. I don't buy any of that 'paradox' theory. You're just another government agent trying to suppress the free market."

"More bullshit."

McAdams's voice grew reasonable. "Look, I bet you're getting paid dick for this mission. Some bureaucrat's salary. My employer can triple it. Quadruple it, even. Just tell me where—"

A bearded figure appeared at the edge of the courtyard, silhouetted in the morning sun. "By the breath of Utuk," Arshan said, "what language are you two speaking? It sounds like goats farting."

McAdams's gun slithered out of sight. "Just an old Greek dialect I picked up. Kyros here found the tablet."

"Of course he did."

"I guess it's time to divvy, then," McAdams said, winking at Kyler.

"Not quite. Iltani isn't here, yet. And I'll need the tablet first, to obtain the full sum …"

As he spoke, a dozen men converged on the courtyard from different directions. Ragged men, lean as hyenas, gripping sickle-bladed swords and knives. Babylonian gutter-trash. They shuffled past Arshan to form a ring around Kyler and McAdams.

"What gives?" the big man said. "I was the one who told you about the buyer. I approached you to set this whole thing up."

"I found a new buyer," Arshan said.

Kyler pulled the copy from his tunic. "What if I just gave you the tablet right now? Would you let us go?"

Arshan shook his head. "Sadly, my new buyer wants no traces on his end. So you'll both have to disappear." He nodded to his cutthroats.

Kyler held the fake high, threatening to break it. But McAdams had already leveled his gun. The automatic barked. Two thugs dropped as explosive bullets tore holes in their chests. The others hesitated, unfamiliar with the strange weapon. McAdams cut down two more while they gawked.

"Clip's dry," he said, in Anglic.

"The secret room." Kyler reached behind the altar and yanked up the concealed trapdoor. Below lay semi-darkness. He leapt down without bothering to use the ladder. McAdams joined him seconds later.

The cedar wood table was still there, and someone had re-lit the lamp. Breathing hard, McAdams glanced at the bright square in the ceiling. "We're trapped in here, you know."

"They can only come at us from one direction."

Above, Arshan's voice exhorted his men to finish the job. Shadows hunched over the trapdoor. McAdams grabbed up the table. He tilted it forward and charged as a trio of men dropped down. Wood slammed them against the wall with bone-jarring force.

"Just like in the ring!" McAdams's shouted. "I'll break your primitive little "

A thug landed on top of him, knife slashing. McAdams hurled the man to the floor. Blood dripped from a deep cut across his pectorals.

Another thug leapt down.

Frowned on or not, Kyler would have to fight, and probably kill, to get out of this alive. He hefted the mace—and caught a faint jingling, behind him. Sharp bronze pressed against his throat.

"Not so fast, handsome," Iltani's voice husked. "Tell me you've got the tablet."

He had to speak carefully, to keep the blade from cutting his Adam's apple. "I've got it. But Arshan will kill you, too."

"Maybe. Maybe not. I'm very persuasive." She took her lips away from his ear. "Ahmose, search him."

A pair of hands felt through his tunic. Kyler could only watch as McAdams fought off three armed men at once. He dislocated a jaw with a single punch, but got a knife in the thigh for his trouble.

The Egyptian eunuch's hands found the tablet and tore it free.

"Alright then," said Iltani. "I've got my bargaining chip. Tell me one good reason why I shouldn't slit your throat right now."

"You have a deep-felt love for humanity?"

The knife bit tighter. "Try again."

"How about this: your eunuch is actually my uncle Damon Cole in disguise, sent back in time from the twenty-third century."

"*What*?"

There was the familiar hiss of a narcoject, and the pressure against Kyler's throat slackened. He turned to see Ahmose/Damon pull a stylus from Iltani's neck. Her rigid body crashed to the floor.

"Your timing, as ever, is impeccable."

Damon tore the veil off his face. Like McAdams, he'd had extra pigmentation implanted. "For your sake, maybe. Not your friend's."

Behind them, McAdams had just finished throttling the last of his attackers. Both men went down in each other's arms. A knife hilt protruded from McAdams's muscled back, near the base of his spine. He convulsed, and a throaty death-rattle filled the chamber.

"*Requiescat in pace*, Big Boss," Kyler said.

"Did you find out who he was working for?"

Kyler shook his head. "The least of our troubles. Arshan's waiting up there and I figure he's still got a couple swordsmen left. We can't activate the recall signal until we've returned the real tablet to Naram Eil."

"Gloom and doom, nephew." Damon fished an egg-shaped object out of his robes. "You really need to put more faith in technology."

"What's that?"

"Gas grenade." A grin split his darkened face. "Non-lethal, but when Arshan and his men wake up they'll have splitting headaches. Too bad aspirin won't be invented for a couple millennia."

†

THE **DRIFTER DETECTIVE** SERIES
FROM BEAT TO A PULP BOOKS

Jack Laramie, grandson of the legendary U.S. Marshal Cash Laramie, is a tough-as-nails WWII vet roaming the modern West. He lives out of a horse trailer hitched to the back of a DeSoto, searching out P.I. gigs to keep him afloat.

THE DRIFTER DETECTIVE | *Garnett Elliott*
HELL UP IN HOUSTON | *Garnett Elliott*
THE GIRLS OF BUNKER PINES | *Garnett Elliott*
WIDE SPOT IN THE ROAD | *Wayne D. Dundee*
DINERO DEL MAR | *Garnett Elliott*
BETWEEN JUAREZ AND EL PASO | *Alec Cizak*
TORN AND FRAYED | *David Cranmer (coming soon)*

THE LAWYER SERIES
FROM BEAT TO A PULP BOOKS

In the Old West, J.D. Miller had been an attorney at law. A respected and successful one. Until the horrific, soul-scarring day when he returned home to find his entire family slaughtered—the charred remains scarcely recognizable in the smoldering ruins of what had once been their house. Like a phoenix rising out of the ashes, The Lawyer—a killing machine—was born, and he's leaving a blood-splattered revenge trail as he searches out those who murdered his family.

STAY OF EXECUTION | *Wayne D. Dundee*
THE RETRIBUTIONERS | *Wayne D. Dundee*
SIX GUNS AT SUNDOWN | *Eric Beetner*
BLOOD MOON | *Eric Beetner (coming soon)*

MORE FROM BEAT TO A PULP BOOKS

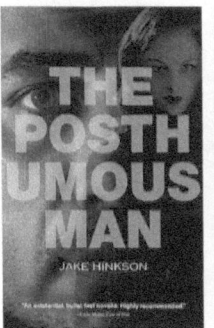

www.beattoapulp.com